JOE
AND THE
KITE

To Joe,

Be Yourself and Shine!.

love

Amanda Humphries
♡

JOE
AND THE
KITE

Amanda Humphries

Matador
9 Priory Business Park,
Wistow Road, Kibworth Beauchamp,
Leicestershire. LE8 0RX
Tel: 0116 279 2299
Email: books@troubador.co.uk
Web: www.troubador.co.uk/matador
Twitter: @matadorbooks

ISBN 978 1838594 015

British Library Cataloguing in Publication Data.
A catalogue record for this book is available from the British Library.

Printed and bound in Great Britain by 4edge Limited
Typeset in 12pt Minion Pro by Troubador Publishing Ltd, Leicester, UK

Matador is an imprint of Troubador Publishing Ltd

I dedicate this book to my family.
"To love and be loved is the greatest gift of all."

Chapter One

Up and Away

Joe looked forward to Saturday; it was the day he got to spend with his dad. They would go to the park and then visit his nan and grandad. Sometimes, as a treat, they would go to the cinema. Joe loved it as Dad always bought him the humongous size popcorn, but he ended up losing half of it as he couldn't resist swinging his legs on the tilted seats. On one particular Saturday, Joe was awoken by the wind whistling through the tiny gap in his open window. His curtains billowed like the sails on a boat.

"Joe, wake up, your dad will be here at half nine, get a wiggle on," shouted his mum up the stairs.

"Coming, Mum," Joe yelled back as he jumped out of bed and glanced in his wardrobe mirror, his brown hair stuck up in all directions. He threw back the curtains of his bedroom window of 27 Leafy Street, Benton Mill; nothing much had changed in nine years. He peered down the garden path below, watching next door's cat hurtling around the lawn and chasing his tail with each gust of wind that blew. He picked up the photo on his windowsill: 'Mum, Dad and Joe at the zoo', it said. Joe had squeezed between his mum and dad on the land train. He smiled at himself; how he had grown since then.

"Hurry up, Joe, your breakfast is getting cold."

"Coming."

Joe didn't want to be late for Dad. Half past nine on the dot he would be there beeping the horn, and Mum going mad if he wasn't ready.

"I hope Dad brings the kite today, it's a great day for flying," said Joe.

"Well, it is a sharp March wind, so maybe, but you will need to wrap up warm, you might get blown away." Mum laughed.

"What, like the time me and Dad went camping? How we didn't lose it I'll never know. It dragged us down the beach for miles!"

"You and your imagination, Joe," said Mum with raised eyebrows.

Joe grinned…

*

At nine thirty sharp, Dad's horn beeped as he drew up by the gate. Joe stood in the hallway and kissed his mum goodbye.

"See you tomorrow, be good for your dad, love you."

"See ya, Mum."

Joe's mum gave the biggest and longest hugs you have ever known, you know, the ones that feel like you might actually get squashed.

It was definitely a day for flying a kite, with the weight of Joe's rucksack hurrying him down the path at full pelt, and the door knocker tapping away behind him.

"Hi, Dad, can we fly the kite today?"

"Alright, Son? Well, that's the plan," answered Dad.

"Yes," muttered Joe under his breath as he high-fived him and put the rucksack in the boot beside the red kite.

"Whatever have you got in here, Joe?" questioned Dad. "It's only for one sleepover."

"Yeah, I know, but Mum has packed us a lunchbox and drinks for later. I've got my clothes, library book… just stuff, Dad," said Joe. Joe's dad nodded and smiled as they sat in the car.

Joe inhaled the smell of the soft, black, leather seats. There was paperwork strewn over the back seats of the car. His dad worked in sales, where he met lots of people. Joe was unsure what his dad did, but he knew it was a demanding job that took him all over the country and away for some nights, so his mum said.

"How did you get on at footy this week?" asked Dad.

"We won 2-1 to Beechfield; Mr Shield said if we win the next two games we've got a good chance of making the final," said Joe.

"Well done, boy, keep giving your best!" said Dad encouragingly as they headed towards the park.

Joe knew every inch of Benton Mill Park: the rusty, black, wrought iron gates through the entrance; the tree-lined pathways around the duck pond; the play area where he used to spend hours being pushed on the swings; and High Point that overlooked the whole of the town.

"Woohoo," shouted Joe as he raced to the top, the chilly wind smacking his rosy cheeks with his collar.

With large, white, fluffy clouds sailing above, Dad looked in all directions. "We need to fly this way," he said as the wind pushed against Joe's rucksack.

"Let me fly first, Dad, it will be easy today," pleaded Joe as Dad began to unravel the kite from its bag.

"You're gonna have to hold on tight, though, Joe, there's quite a wind speed," Dad instructed.

Joe held the red handle, unravelling the string as

Dad backed up and held the kite above his head. Joe felt the force against the kite as if it were fighting its way free. Just like walking Grandad's dog, Sam, or rather, Sam walking Joe.

"I'm ready!" yelled Joe as his words got lost in the melody of the wind blowing a gale. "Let go." Dad released the kite as Joe ran forward, battling to keep his grip and the kite under control; with its height gaining quickly, Joe released more string. The red kite ascended into the bright blue sky beyond.

"It's pulling me forward, I can't stop!" Joe laughed, as his little legs couldn't keep up. Suddenly he felt his feet leave the ground.

"Joe!" Dad shouted, grasping at the heel of his shoe as it pulled away from his fingers.

"Get me, Dad," screamed Joe as the powerful gust pulled him higher and tears streamed down his face from the biting wind around him. Joe looked back to see his dad fading into the distance, his arms waving frantically as Joe looked down above the treetops. His fearful screams were silenced by this giant force of nature that took his every breath. With the park below him, Joe kept gaining height, his clothes flapping frantically around.

Looking at the kite above, it appeared hidden within a mass of white cloud. Swirling, twirling, spinning; Joe was caught in the centre of a blank white canvas. Dizzy and afraid, he gripped hard on the little red handle, squinting his eyes at the bright, white light around.

"Ow," shouted Joe as he fell to the ground with a bump, rubbing his eyes to see. But this wasn't the park; where was he?

Chapter Two

Cloud Land

Following the string with his eyes, Joe spotted his red kite on the ground beside a tree. Gazing and feeling the smooth, white, shiny surface beneath him, he got up. His nose twitched at the strong aroma of flowers or something like what his mum was always spraying when she was going out. Where was he? Putting down his rucksack, Joe surveyed his surroundings. It was like some sort of castle grounds. Beyond the white, glassy floor were grass, trees, flowers and a giant wall surrounding it. Joe shielded his eyes from the bright sunlight above as sweat started to trickle down his face.

"It's a bit warm," Joe said to himself, stripping off his coat and shoving it in his rucksack…

Gulping back his orange juice in the warm sunshine, he noticed there was hardly a breeze. Could the wind have blown him far from Benton Mill and to some old castle far away? Joe looked around; there wasn't a sign of anyone. Just quiet, the sound of a few birds whistling, and, strangely, leaves rustling on the trees. But there weren't any in the park; this looked more like summer, so where exactly was Joe? Walking towards his kite, Joe could hear sobbing sounds coming from an overgrown bush covered in bright pink flowers.

"Mum! Dad! Mum! Dad!" the tearful voice cried out. Behind the bush, huddled on the grass, was a girl; her wavy blonde hair covered her face as she looked down. Joe stared as he realised she obviously hadn't heard him through her cries, her hand gripped tightly to a green handle with string.

Crouching down, he tapped the arm of her purple jacket. Her curls revealed a pale, freckle-faced stare and her blue eyes widened as she let out the loudest scream. You know, like girls often do when being chased around the playground at break time.

"It's OK, I won't hurt you," said Joe, trying to calm the girl down.

"Who are you? Where am I?" said the frightened face looking at Joe, wiping the tears from her swollen eyes.

"I'm Joe, I don't know where we are. One minute I was flying my kite in the park with my dad, and the next, I got blown away in a whirlwind to here, wherever that is!"

The girl looked around – "Where is this? Where's my mum and dad?" – as tears started to build up like pools in her eyes.

"I don't know, but we'll find out, I'm sure there's a good explanation," Joe said, trying to sound reassuring. He held out his hand to pull her up.

"I'm Ellie," she said, standing to her feet and looking at the green kite handle still in her grip. "My kite." Ellie grabbed at the green kite string, pulling and pulling until, there in one perfect piece, it sat like a puppy dog by her side. Ellie looked around. "It's a castle, we are in the castle grounds, just like the one we went to yesterday. We are in Wales, then," she declared.

"How do you know that?" asked Joe, a puzzled look appearing on his face.

"Well, there are lots of castles, and we have visited most of them, I don't think this one, though. We were on holiday in Wales – I mean, me, my mum and dad and my little sister, Grace. We were on the beach and it was very windy; I held the kite. Sand was blowing everywhere. I just couldn't stop running as it pulled me, then I went up in the air and couldn't get down. They shouted, 'Let go,' but I was too scared to fall. It was high. I saw a big, white cloud, then I was dizzy, and it was bright, and I fell down here," explained Ellie.

"Well, if we are in Wales, then why are there leaves on the trees and it's hot like summer but it's March?" Joe questioned.

Ellie and Joe left their kites beside the bush to explore. Ellie tied her jacket around her waist as they squinted their eyes to protect them from the bright sunlight and sea blue sky. They shared the picnic that Mum had packed for Joe and his dad.

*

Behind the bush, and far from view, he stood watching them, bending down to pick up the red and green kites. A smile spreading across his white, bearded face. He turned towards his blue-feathered friend who took the kites, her female body clothed in feathers, like a beautiful bird, gentle but strong.

"Mr Iam," she said, her hand resting on her hip, "shall I put these with the others?"

He nodded, gazing back at the children as they searched along the wall for the exit:

> "A boy and girl to play the game,
> to win will send them home again,
> but if they lose then they will see,
> forever they will live with me."

His words echoed as Octavia walked away clutching the kites. With that, he was gone...

*

"There must be a way out somewhere," said Ellie.

"Of course there is, we will speak to the person working here and they can come and get us," Joe replied.

"Funny, we haven't seen anyone yet," said Ellie.

The children headed towards a pathway in the middle of the gardens that was surrounded by a pool. "It must be getting late by now, Mum and Dad will be worried and Grace will be howling," said Ellie.

"That's strange," Joe said, frowning. "My watch says quarter past ten, but it can't be, my dad picked me up at half past nine and it was about ten o'clock when we got to High Point to fly the kite. We have been here ages!"

"Well, it probably stopped when you bumped on the ground," Ellie suggested.

The children followed the path around the pool, then it veered left, then right, heading in different directions. Beyond the right path, behind the trees, stood the castle, its grey turrets pointing above the white stony pillars.

"There, told you it was a castle," Ellie announced. "We'll follow this path, look, it goes through the trees and the castle is just there." As they headed along the path to the right, there stood an old, white-haired, bearded man facing them.

Chapter Three

Out of Time

Approaching the tall, bearded man, Joe and Ellie were relieved to see someone to help them find their way back home. Towering above them, and wearing a medieval robe, he smiled without saying a word.

"Excuse me, is this the way to the castle exit? You see, we need to get back, I mean, find out where our families are," said Joe. The man just smiled.

"Are we still in Wales?" questioned Ellie, holding the sleeve of Joe's jumper that was tied around his waist as she hovered behind him. The man just looked at them, his eyes staring, kind but intense. It was like time had just stopped. Just like the pause button on the TV, the scene was still, as Joe and Ellie waited for the man to speak.

"You've come up to this land of mine, where there is no such thing as time. Mr Iam is my name and both of you will play the game."

Joe and Ellie looked at each other. A land outside of time. What was this place?

Mr Iam just smiled. "Just follow me and have no fear, everything will be made clear." Mr Iam's words seemed to echo as he turned around to lead the way. Joe and Ellie gripped each other's arms as they followed him.

"I'm scared, Joe, I want to go home," Ellie stuttered.

"So do I," replied Joe. "But we haven't got a choice. I don't have a clue where this place is, but unless we follow him, what hope have we got of getting back home?"

Approaching the towering oak door, Mr Iam placed his hand over the wrought iron pattern. Instantly it opened to a courtyard. He beckoned the children through.

"Where is the door handle, Joe? How did he do that?" Ellie asked, frowning. Joe shrugged his shoulders and shook his head, looking as puzzled as Ellie. The children stepped into the courtyard as the door shut behind them. Mr Iam walked towards a seating area on the grass. There sat, as if waiting for them, a beautiful woman. Well, a bird-like woman – with soft blue and black feathers, like clothes, but actually skin – beaming a bright smile. She stood as she hugged Mr Iam. Then, while kissing his hand, she flung her arm back as if leading him to sit down. Joe and Ellie just stood there, this blue-feathered being before them.

"Welcome, welcome, you must be tired from your travels. I've made some refreshments – cup of tea, anyone?" she said as the children looked at the white-tabled delight before them. She poured them tea into flowery cups, assuming that was what they always drank. The table was full of every kind of cake you could imagine and ones that Joe and Ellie had never seen before.

"Sorry, first things first, you are?" she asked, standing up again and reaching her arms out towards them.

"I'm Joe, this is Ellie, and I want to know exactly where we are, and who you are," he said, pointing to Mr Iam. "What did you mean, no such thing as time and a game to play? Is this some sort of strange dream place?" Joe asked abruptly.

"Listen, listen," replied the woman, with one hand on her hip and one on Joe's shoulder. "You didn't choose to come here and we didn't choose to have you, but you have been brought here for a reason. Your land must have sent you. I'm Octavia, Mr Iam's assistant, teashop owner and a Whodin, of course," she said proudly, leading the children by the hand to sit between her and Mr Iam.

"A Whodin, what's a Whodin?" asked Ellie, sipping at her strange green-coloured tea.

"All in good time. Now, anyone for cake?" said Octavia, cutting a piece covered with strawberry jam and flower petals. Joe shuddered as he sipped the bitter, warm drink, glancing over at Mr Iam, who didn't seem to take his eyes off him. You know,

that kind of stare the teacher gives you when you're talking, and you should be getting on with your work.

The sun was beaming between the turrets of the castle roofs and glistened on the flowery tea set as they all ate and drank. Joe and Ellie were pretending that all was fine when they were actually scared of what was going to happen to them.

Finishing his tea, Mr Iam cleared his throat as he stood. Joe and Ellie watched his every move. He had this strange, powerful presence that could be felt all around him.

"I am the ruler of Cloud Land, where everything I've made by hand. Where you can't age and time stands still, and no one ever will get ill. But you must follow by my rules, or you will end up being fools. For if you choose to go astray, then consequences come your way." His voice echoed as he began to walk away towards the steps leading into the castle.

"Wait a minute," shouted Joe. "Why have we both been sent here? You said we had a game to play, what is that to do with anything? We just want to go home."

Octavia put her arms around the children as Ellie began to cry. "There, there, all will be OK," she said reassuringly.

As the children walked towards the steps, following Octavia, the air filled with one long blast of the sound of a horn.

"What is that?" Joe and Ellie said in unison.

Octavia turned, carrying the tea tray. "Mr Iam has called for a meeting in the village. Now, everyone must go, including me. I will be back when light turns to dark," she said, walking through the open doorway.

Ellie turned around, watching the sun setting in the distance as the door closed behind her. Joe followed Octavia through the castle entrance. The air was filled with the fresh fragrance of fruit, not the usual old dusty smells that castles have. Doorways led off the grand entrance hall as Octavia left her tray on a table to lead the children up the vast, wooden spiral staircase.

"You can rest here a while, there is a washroom through that door, but you cannot leave the room until Mr Iam comes for you. When dark comes, just touch the button for light. I will bring back some food, I've made a big soup. Toodle-loo," said Octavia as she locked the door. Joe put his rucksack on one of the beds as Ellie looked out of the window. Looking down on the courtyard below, she noticed the castle walls beyond, and what seemed like a dark forest in the distance, as the light was growing dim. How could Joe and Ellie rest? They questioned this weird world they had found themselves in…

*

After finishing their vegetable soup at the table in the corner of the room, Mr Iam opened the door and placed a rolled-up scroll in front of them. Joe unravelled it to reveal a map. He glanced at the drawing as Ellie pointed to the castle.

"Look, we're here," she said.

Mr Iam looked at the children with a kind but serious look on his face. "After sleep, when light has come, then your game will have begun," he said.

"What game?" asked Joe.

"Why have we got to play a game? I just want to go home," pleaded Ellie.

"If you want to get back home, you can't do it on your own. You must solve the riddles together, or you will stay here forever. To face your fears and overcome, now your journey has begun. Bring all the objects back to me, and then the wind will set you free. But on the right path you must stay, a Whodin to help you on the way. Who is friend? Who is foe? Who can you trust? How will you know? Now you must follow by my rules, or you will end up being fools." Then, he handed them an envelope and closed the door behind him.

Chapter Four

The First Riddle

Ellie ran her finger across the seal and pulled out the card. On one side, there was a list of ten rules from Mr Iam.

"We have to read this and learn it, Ellie," said Joe. "I don't want to find out what the consequences might be." Joe and Ellie each held a corner of the card as they read out the rules to follow:

Mr Iam's Rules

1. Mr Iam is ruler of Cloud Land; he made everything.
2. Always tell the truth.
3. Don't take anything that isn't yours.
4. Love and respect everyone.
5. Be kind and helpful to everyone.
6. Never hurt anyone.

7. Work hard at what you do to earn a living.
8. Be happy with what you have. Don't wish for other people's things.
9. Eat a balanced diet, exercise and sleep well.
10. Don't forget your manners; always say yes please or no thank you.

"Well, these are some of my class's golden rules," Joe said confidently.

"I don't think they are difficult to follow, just be good and kind," replied Ellie. "Mr Iam is the only person that can help us to get on our way back home, this is his land. Who are the Whodins? Octavia said she was one. Does that mean they are all bird-like people? Do you think there are any normal people like us, Joe?"

"I don't know, but we'll soon find out. Mr Iam is human, sort of, even though he can magic doors open, make everything, speak only in rhymes and goodness knows what else!" said Joe, raising his eyebrows. He turned the card over to reveal the first riddle:

> *"To solve the riddle, find the clue,*
> *you must follow what to do,*
> *to walk by trust and not by sight,*
> *will turn the darkness into light."*

Joe turned to Ellie. "Teamwork, we can solve the riddles, get all the objects and get back home. We will do it, Ellie, but we have to stick together," said Joe.

"I know, and face our fears, maybe that is why we have both been sent here, to learn together. What are you scared of, Joe?" Ellie asked.

"I'm not scared of anything," Joe said, opening up the map again to have a look.

"Are you telling the truth? That's one of the rules," said Ellie, frowning.

Joe's head turned quickly to look her in the eye. "Um, well not very much," he said, keeping his thoughts to himself. The children sat to study the map. This land outside of time went far beyond the castle walls. But how would they know if they were going to stay on the right path?

"I think we need to head to The House of Light," said Joe, pointing. "That should give us the clue."

*

When light had come, after a much-needed sleep, Joe and Ellie tucked into the breakfast Octavia had set before them. It was an unusual breakfast. There were small bread rolls shaped like mini footballs; a huge bowl of porridge-type cereal; mountains of fruits; and on the side were honeycomb-like sweets but in the shape of a comb; milk; and fruit juice. It was quite a feast. Joe rubbed his stomach as he looked at the riddle again.

"We have to walk where dark will turn to light. Look, if we follow the path through the woods from the castle, and past the mill and granary," he said, pointing on the map, "there it says, 'The House of Light' – our clue must be there." Ellie nodded.

*

Octavia stopped as they reached the end of the drawbridge over the moat. "Listen, listen, you have the map, you have the riddle, follow the right way, and you will find it, but be careful who you trust," she said, pointing her feathered finger at them then up to her closed lips, just like a teacher might do to get the class to be quiet.

"How will we know who the Whodins are to help us?" Ellie asked.

"Oh, you will, Ellie, remember, follow the rules," Octavia said, her arm on Ellie's shoulder.

"Where are all the riddles?" asked Joe.

"One at a time now, don't be impatient, it's a game you have to finish, Joe," she said, with her hands on her hips. "I'm off to the teashop, so toodle-loo." Octavia embraced the children, patted Joe's rucksack and turned to go back across the drawbridge.

Following the map, the children headed on a pathway leading down through a wood, with the castle well behind them. The shade of the giant trees was a relief from the heat of the sun. Everything seemed quite normal: birds whistling, leaves rustling and a gentle breeze. Ellie nervously turned on her heels every now and again to check there was no one behind them. Climbing over the stile, they headed across the field towards the mill as the river ran beside them. Sitting on the riverbank, two figures turned to look and got up. It was a bird-like man, clothed in black feathers, with shiny, swept-back, feathered hair; and a man with the features of a rat, with big, pink, sticky-out ears and a tail. Joe and Ellie froze as they walked towards them.

"Lost your way?" said the bird-man, pointing to their map. "Maybe we can help you."

"Are you a Whodin?" Ellie asked.

A slow smile spread across the rat-man's face. "What a question, Boss," the rat-man said to his companion.

"Now, how should you come to ask us that?" muttered the bird-man.

"Octavia said that Whodins are helpers," replied Ellie.

"Oh yes, they help alright," replied the rat-man as he started to chuckle and tap-dance with his feet.

Joe looked at Ellie and put his finger to his closed lips.

"You must be looking for Mr Grainger, he runs the mill, just over there, a very good Whodin," said the rat-man.

"Shut it, Winston," interrupted the bird-man.

"OK, Boss," the rat-man replied as he dropped his head.

"I'm Caiden and this is Winston. We are, well, friends of Octavia, you could say. You are little people finding your way, no doubt, with your map in hand. I'm sure you are needing some help, so it's good you found us."

Joe and Ellie had no choice but to go along with the two strange creatures, unsure if they should trust them or if they were actually Whodins at all.

Walking towards the mill, Joe pulled the riddle from the side pocket of his rucksack. It wouldn't be long before they reached The House of Light. In the distance was a towering white building; the beacon was high above the treetops, like the one on the map.

"What have you there?" Caiden asked, peering over Joe's shoulder, looking intrigued. Joe stopped in his tracks, facing Caiden and Winston. Taking the map from Ellie, he revealed very little about their strange arrival into Cloud Land and about following the rules and riddles to get them home again. Joe had to tell the truth, but could he trust them?

As the children reached their destination, they watched as the water cascaded over the mill wheel and down into the stream below.

"Is this where you work?" Ellie asked, turning to Winston.

Caiden glared at Winston as he paused to reply. "I used to, but not anymore. We've got our own business now, hey, Boss?" Winston said. Caiden elbowed him, the red-faced rat-man's smile turning sad.

Just then a door opened from the side of the granary as three workers came down the steps, carrying what seemed like bags of grain. Caiden and Winston waved as they hurried their way towards them, forgetting the children left behind.

"Come on, Ellie, I'm not sure we can trust they are Whodins, let's follow this dirt track, The House of Light is only over there," Joe said hurriedly.

'The House of Light', said the sign at the bottom of the tiny path. Walking towards the door, Joe and Ellie heard harp music coming from inside.

"That sounds nice, Joe," Ellie said, spinning around and waving her arms like a ballerina.

"I hope this is the right place for the clue, Ellie, this is the light place, but I'm not sure about the darkness," Joe said, reading the riddle again:

> *"To solve the riddle, find the clue,*
> *you must follow what to do,*
> *to walk by trust and not by sight,*
> *will turn the darkness into light."*

He knocked on the little red door.

Chapter Five

Into the Darkness

The harp music stopped, and footsteps were heard coming towards the door. It opened and there stood a vision of white, her beautiful dress, sparkling like diamonds, draped to the floor.

"Hello, I'm Clarissa. I've been expecting you, do come in," she said, in a calm, gentle voice. Joe and Ellie entered the small, round building. The room filled with light shining down from above, so bright that they could hardly look up. There were two small windows with cushioned seats underneath and standing prominent as a centrepiece was a beautiful harp.

"Take a seat," Clarissa said as she poured the children some milk. "You must be thirsty after your long walk." She placed a plate of biscuits before them.

"How did you know we were coming?" Joe asked her, looking puzzled.

"Mr Iam, of course."

"So, you must be a Whodin, then. He said they will help us," commented Ellie.

"Yes, I am," replied Clarissa.

"So, what is a Whodin?" Joe responded.

"Everyone that follows Mr Iam's rules. He rules over this land because he made it; he made us. Everything is good – well, it was, until some decided they had had enough of following him and chose to go their own way. Now they live with the consequences," Clarissa said.

"Yeah, we heard about those, what are they?" asked Joe, with a worried expression.

"Just solve your riddles together, Joe, but stick to the rules. The Whodins will help you and your conscience will let you know right from wrong. I can't say any more." And with that, she walked across the room. On the wall was a large, round, gold button. She pressed it, and unravelling itself from the brightness above, a tall, golden ladder appeared.

"Wow!" shouted Ellie. "That's clever, where does that go?"

Standing on the bottom rung, Clarissa turned to the children. "My job is a light bearer. When dark comes, everyone needs light to see. Mr Iam has enough up here for every Whodin. One light would normally cost one token. But your light is free, a gift, he said, as you have to pass the test." With that, she began to climb up the ladder.

They watched as she went higher and higher into the distance and out of view. Joe and Ellie sat there, puzzled. What were tokens? What had happened to the ones who chose not to be Whodins anymore? Winston had said he used to work for Mr Grainger at the Mill, but he and Caiden had got their own business. Was it a good one? Caiden wasn't very kind to Winston, either. Joe and Ellie were convinced that they couldn't be Whodins at all and wouldn't trust them if they saw them again.

Ellie couldn't resist following Clarissa up the golden ladder. As she started her ascent, she called for Joe to follow her. Immediately, the rungs collapsed and she fell to the ground.

"Ouch, that hurt!" Ellie moaned.

"They are not meant for you to climb, then," replied Joe as the rungs appeared in their right place again. Picking herself up, Ellie looked around to see a small, round, brass hook attached to the floor. Looking, she called Joe over to see.

"It looks like a trap-door hatch to me," said Joe as his finger traced over the outline. "Let's wait until Clarissa gets back to ask her what it is. She is really nice and will help us. If she is getting us a light, then it's probably a torch, and I bet we have to go somewhere dark to use it, that will be the test," said Joe as fear spread across Ellie's face.

"I hate the dark, I have to have my lamp on when I go to sleep," said Ellie, her voice breaking off into gasps as she started to cry.

Joe put his arm around her. "Ellie, if we don't pass this, then we don't get to go home." He went to get a tissue out of his rucksack as Clarissa was making her way back down the ladder.

"There," she said, handing the light to Joe. His predictions were right. Ellie looked at the torch while wiping her tears with the tissue. "I can see this riddle was intended for you then, Ellie. Just keep following the light, it will lead you out of the darkness." She bent down to give her a hug.

The room filled with the peaceful sound of Clarissa playing her harp as the children finished their milk and biscuits.

"Before I take you to the right path, if you need the bathroom, it's here." Clarissa lifted the little brass hook, pulling back the floor.

"We wondered what that was for," said Joe.

Stepping down into an underground hallway, she led the way. Leading them through the back door of The House of Light and through her flower-scented garden, Clarissa showed the children the pathway to take.

"Follow this path and stay on it, you will come to the entrance of the tunnel. You have to keep going through it until you come out the other side. Mr Iam will be waiting." Joe put the torch in his rucksack as they said goodbye.

Following the well-worn path through the edge of a meadow, Joe looked up at the white, fluffy clouds above.

"I wonder if they are different lands too or just normal clouds?" he said, the breeze cooling the children as they walked.

"You mean there could be other worlds like this one? Maybe. Well, this seems a nice place to live if you never get poorly or old," Ellie replied.

"Imagine only being nine forever," said Joe.

"Or eight," Ellie butted in. "You never get the chance to be a grown-up, how boring!" Ellie skipped ahead, waving her arms around like a dance. Joe looked at the map again, his eyes following the pathway from The House of Light; the path would take them through the fields, heading back towards the river.

Ellie, immersed in her dancing world, failed to see Winston crouched by a tree, holding a box filled with berries.

"Hey, Ellie, where are you off to? Good to see ya!" Winston stood, his hand reaching out to shake hers.

Ellie screamed as Winston frowned, his ears pointing, startled. Joe ran towards them.

"I won't hurt you, why would I?" replied Winston, his whiskers twitching as he spoke.

"You… you're not a Whodin, are you?" Joe said, his voice slightly shaking.

"Course I am, I'm being nice, aren't I?" Winston started to eat the berries, scoffing them like he hadn't eaten in ages.

"You must be hungry; do you want one of our sandwiches that Clarissa made?" Ellie said. Joe glared at Ellie, putting his finger to his lips.

Winston shared their lunch as they sat by the tree. Just then, the sound of the horn filled the air, but Winston didn't move to Mr Iam's call to meeting.

"We've got to go now, bye then." Joe got up, grabbing Ellie by the arm as she picked up the sandwich box and drinks. "Mr Iam is waiting for us," said Joe.

The furry rat-man, who sat finishing his sandwich, saluted them. Joe looked at Winston's black, stripy waistcoat. There was a badge with the letter 'C' on it. Exactly the same badge that Caiden was wearing on his long, black, feathered jacket.

Joe and Ellie hurried along the path, hearing the rushing water heading downstream.

"He most definitely is not a Whodin, that proved it, Ellie. He didn't go to the meeting Mr Iam called. Octavia said everyone goes, Winston didn't budge, did he?" Joe stated.

"You're right," replied Ellie.

With the tunnel up ahead of them, Joe reached

for the torch, pressing the button to check it was working. Ellie started to cry.

"We can do this, Ellie, you won't be scared, I'm giving you the torch to hold, and my hand will hold your other one. We'll keep walking till we get to the other side. Just keep focusing on this getting us on our way back home."

Ellie scrunched up her face and, with determination, took hold of the torch, as she grabbed Joe's hand. The entrance was wide, but as they looked in, darkness lurked beyond. Joe sniffed in the damp, earthy air and, side by side, they entered the tunnel. Ellie gripped Joe's hand tightly. As the light grew dimmer behind them, the little, bright torch lit the path that lay before them. The sound of dripping water echoed as they reached deep into the dark tunnel. Ellie felt something brush past her head; as she ducked she dropped the torch. Joe reached down to pick up the light as Ellie screamed.

"What touched my head?" Her words were repeated by an echo.

"Probably just a bat." Joe shone the torch around. Ellie, now grabbing hold of Joe's arm, tightly shut her eyes. "Just bats, look." Ellie opened her eyes, looking at the light. The bats were hanging from the top of the tunnel. "We can't stop, we must keep moving." Joe pulled Ellie along. A pinhead of light appearing in the distance. The children picked up pace as they made their way to the end, the light growing brighter.

"We did it!" yelled Ellie, jumping up and down. "Thanks for helping me, Joe."

But no one was there to meet them.

Chapter Six

The Second Riddle

As they looked around, not knowing which way to go next, Ellie noticed some sort of white lake in the distance. Heading towards it, the children wondered where Mr Iam was, as Clarissa had said he would meet them at the end of the tunnel. A wooden sign said, 'The Milk Lake'.

"Is that really milk?" Ellie asked.

Joe bent down and reached over the still, white pool. Cupping his hands, he scooped some up, smelling it first. "It's milk alright, and it's cool."

"Brilliant," said Ellie, leaning over and taking some for herself. "How did that get in there? It's just like it's out of the fridge." The children's faces were smeared in white as they laughed at each other. Mr Iam, watching them, smiled as he walked in their direction. In his hand was the envelope to the second riddle.

Spotting him, they got up. "Mr Iam, we have found the clue." Joe beamed, and then got the torch out of his rucksack to show him.

"It was really scary in the tunnel, but I did it!" Ellie declared, punching her arm in the air.

"You faced your fear to overcome, you passed that test and you have won, but keep the object safe for me, it's all of them I need to see." He handed Ellie the little brown envelope, and with that, he was gone.

"To solve the riddle, find the clue,
you must follow what to do,
north or south, east or west,
which direction is the best?"

Joe and Ellie studied the second riddle.

"How are we going to know which direction is the best?" asked Joe. "Or which way is north or south? Hang on, my dad says the sun always sets to the west. We must be facing south because the sun is going down over there," Joe said, pointing.

"We have to stay on the right path, Joe. We need a Whodin. I wish Clarissa was here, she would help us," replied Ellie, looking at the map.

The children headed towards the pathway again. Soon it would be dark and both of them, feeling tired from the journey, needed a place to rest.

"If we carry on south for just a short way it says 'Activity Village', there must be somewhere there we can stop and get help," Ellie said, rolling the map back up.

Joe reached for the torch as the light started to fade, the pathway leading the children on a wide dirt track.

"Joe, we have to get to the village before it's dark, I'm scared," said Ellie, panicking.

"We're OK, we have the light to show us the way. Don't worry, we will soon be there."

But would they? Dark was fast approaching. Both of them felt alone, unsure if this was the right path at all. Up ahead, a dark figure appeared to be stood in the distance. Joe shone his torch; it flickered in the twilight sky as the stars twinkled above. Gripped with fear, the children edged their way towards it. 'Which Way Crossroads', said the tall wooden outpost.

"Where are we now?" asked Ellie, hanging onto Joe's arm.

"How do I know?" Joe snapped back. "I'm not the grown-up."

Ellie started to get upset. "I want to go home," she cried as Joe grew more flustered by them being lost and shone the torch in all directions. 'Whistle Top Mountains to the left, Activity Village to the right, Whodin Town straight ahead', it said. The only light to see was shining towards the direction of the village.

Hanging from the branches of the tree-lined path, lanterns were lighting up around them as they walked past the quaint little rows of terraced cottages, the lights shining from their windows.

"I wonder what activities the village does?" asked Ellie, calmer now that they had reached what seemed a safer place.

"Let's find out," Joe answered. The children walked towards a large building with lights shining from the numerous windows around it.

Walking down the corridor, there seemed a busyness in the air, with the sound of voices chatting, whooping and cheering. Then a round of applause could be heard. Joe and Ellie peered through the small glass porthole in the door, standing on tiptoes to see.

"Hey, it's five-a-side," Joe said, excitedly watching. The room was full of players and spectators. "Let's go in." Before Ellie had chance to reply, Joe pushed open the door.

Just then, a whistle blew for half-time. Joe and Ellie stood staring at the strangeness of the people around the room. Some beings were animal people like Octavia, Caiden and Winston, and others were just like Clarissa and Mr Iam. Male and female, but no children in sight. Silence fell as heads turned towards the door. Joe and Ellie huddled together.

"Little people, where did you come from?" said a voice out of the crowd, watching.

Joe swallowed hard, preparing himself to speak. "We are Joe and Ellie, and we're trying to find the right way." Joe pulled the riddle out of his back pocket. "Mr Iam sent us."

Just then, everyone stood to their feet and began to clap for them. A man from one of the teams walked towards them. His long, dark hair was tied up in a knot; a smile spread across his brown-bearded face. He put his hand out to shake. "You have come to the right place then. I'm Mr Bun, the football coach, and the baker of Whodin town. Fancy a game?"

Before Joe had time to think, he was playing football for the red team.

Ellie sat on the bench holding Joe's rucksack as a woman that had the features of a black and white cat came to sit next to her. Her ears were sticking out from a black, furry sort of hat and her black tail was swiping the air, then curling itself around her.

"Hi Ellie, I'm Purdy," said the cat-woman, her voice beginning to purr after she spoke. "What activity do you want to do?"

Ellie paused. "What is there? I'm not that keen on football, but I do like to dance. I do ballet and after-school art club."

"What's art club?" enquired Purdy.

"Oh, you know, painting, drawing, stuff like that," said Ellie, with a puzzled look on her face.

"Do you want to come and see the other activities?" she asked.

"Um, yes, but I'll wait for Joe first if that's OK?"

"Sure, is there anything I can help you with?" asked the cat-woman, her green eyes slowly blinking.

"You are a Whodin, aren't you?" asked Ellie.

"We are all Whodins here," she replied.

Just then the whistle blew for full-time. Ellie made her way towards Joe.

"We won 1-0!" shouted Joe, his face beaming, as he was the youngest player on the team.

As the team dispersed, Mr Bun and Purdy gave them a guided tour. There were lots of rooms leading off the corridor; one was like a dance studio with mirrors on the wall. Another had musical instruments on a stage. One was like a library. All the rooms seemed to be for different activities.

As they reached the end of the corridor, a voice called out behind them. "Joe and Ellie, at last you made it."

Everyone turned as a pink flamingo bird-man stood in front of them, wearing a ballet dancer's tutu, his pink, spindly, long legs stood straight like a tall statue. As he came forward to greet them, he jangled a large bunch of keys.

"This is Mr Gimbal, the dance teacher. He is in charge of the activity centre. I'm just showing them around," said Mr Bun.

"Mr Gimbal, are you the Whodin to help us?" Joe asked.

"That's right," he replied. Bending down, he curtsied, throwing his arms back up to a graceful pose, his keys clanking. "Come with me," he said, pirouetting around and heading through the door.

"See you, Ellie, meet me at the dance class," Purdy said, giving a little wave as she left.

Ellie beamed. "Great, thanks, Purdy, see you then, hopefully."

Mr Gimbal locked the door behind him, heading down the moonlit path with Joe, Ellie and Mr Bun. Joe yawned as he put his rucksack over his shoulder. Saying goodbye to Mr Bun, they followed Mr Gimbal to the first terraced house.

After supper, Joe took the riddle from his pocket.

"Are we heading in the right direction? You knew we were coming, Mr Iam must have told you," said Joe, questioning Mr Gimbal. Crossing his long, spindly legs, he placed the object on the table in front of them.

Chapter Seven

Lost and Found

"Of course, a compass. That tells you the direction you are going in," said Joe, holding it in his hand.

"What is the whistle on it for?" asked Ellie, taking it from Joe.

"That's how you call for transportation, one long blow will bring it to you," Mr Gimbal replied.

"What transportation?" Joe asked, looking puzzled.

"If you don't want to walk or you need to go far, one long whistle and it will come and pick you up and take you. You will see better when light comes. Now, I'll show you to your rooms." Mr Gimbal's pink, stripy pyjamas covered his long, skinny legs as he led the way up the steep cottage stairs.

*

Ellie walked into Joe's room, rubbing her hair dry with a towel.

"We must have slept for hours, I needed that," said Ellie as Joe was combing his hair in the mirror.

"That's just it, there isn't time here at all. Just day and night, or light and dark, as they seem to call it. It's strange not having a clock or watch," Joe stated.

"How does everyone know when things happen, like dance class?" replied Ellie.

"Not sure, a horn for this, a whistle for that, maybe a drum roll," Joe said, sniggering as the children laughed.

Finishing up their breakfast, there was a knock at the cottage door. Mr Gimbal lifted the latch.

"Clarissa," yelled the children. Her radiance filled the room as she handed Mr Gimbal a parcel.

"Hello, you two, what a nice surprise seeing you again," she said softly as they stood up to greet her.

"Mr Gimbal had our second clue," said Ellie, grinning.

"You made it through the darkness, then?" Clarissa declared.

"They know they are going the right way," responded Mr Gimbal as he brushed his pink, feathery tracksuit arms.

"Yes, we did, then we were lost, not really knowing which way to go, but we found it," said Joe.

"You followed the right path, then," said Clarissa. Joe and Ellie nodded.

Mr Gimbal took three little lights out of the box, placing them on the table. Taking from his pocket a little drawstring bag, he handed Clarissa three golden marbles. "Thank you," she said. "I'll see you later after work when I have my music class." Saying goodbye to the children, she left.

"Come on then," said Mr Gimbal. "I have work to do and I would like you to help me, please."

Joe and Ellie followed the flamingo-man back to the activity centre. With no sign of Mr Iam for the next riddle, they would have to do some work.

Reaching into the back of the cupboard, Mr Gimbal produced two blue overalls for the children. They put them on over their clothes and rolled back the sleeves. Joe looked in the mirror on the storeroom wall.

"How come you have children's clothes? We haven't seen any other children here yet," he said while turning up the hems over his trainers.

"Children, what are they?" asked Mr Gimbal, preening his feathers in the mirror behind Joe.

"Little people, you seem to call us," replied Ellie.

"Oh, little people. No, we don't have little people here. Well, we have had little people, but not anymore. They came and they disappeared. No one seemed to see them again," said Mr Gimbal.

Ellie looked at Joe, frowning.

Cloud Land, a place full of grown-ups. But where did the children come from? More to the point, where did they disappear to?

Joe and Ellie set to work, dusting, sweeping and mopping as hard as they could to get all the jobs done, helping Mr Gimbal have every room ready for the activities.

Joe rubbed his back as he helped to finish putting up the last bouncy castle in the jumping room.

"Right, anyone hungry?" asked Mr Gimbal, passing the children a lunchbox each. "We'll eat outside."

Sitting on the warm grass, the tree gave some shade as the three workers stopped to eat. Looking into the horizon, above the rooftops, Joe could see something white heading towards them.

"What's that coming?" Joe asked, pointing in the sky.

"It's probably Flora bringing my fresh flowers from her shop, or to sort her books in the book room," Mr Gimbal answered. Floating peacefully, the giant white feather landed on the grass in front of them. The blonde-haired, flowery lady stepped off, carrying a basket of flowers and a large red book tucked under her arm. She blew the whistle attached to a string around her neck, just like the one Joe and Ellie now had. With that, the huge white feather lifted off the ground and whoosh, it was gone.

"Oh, my goodness, little people," she said, bending down to Joe and Ellie and holding out her hand.

Joe and Ellie sat with mouths wide open at what had just occurred.

"Flora, Ellie. Ellie, Flora. Flora, Joe. Joe, Flora," said Mr Gimbal, his head turning side to side. You know, like when spectators are engrossed watching a tennis match. Everyone laughed.

Enjoying their warm, sunny break, the children lay on the grass, tired from their hard work, laughing spontaneously as Flora and Mr Gimbal shared with them some funny stories. Joe and Ellie put their four golden marbles each into their pockets as Mr Gimbal thanked them for their hard work.

"What can we do with marbles, I mean, tokens?" asked Joe.

"Use them for whatever you want, an exchange for something. You have earned them, it's up to you. Every Whodin works and collects their tokens from Franklin in the town. He runs The Token Bank for Mr Iam. They can exchange them with whatever they want," Mr Gimbal replied.

Joe smiled as he looked across at Ellie cartwheeling across the grass. "Don't lose your tokens," shouted Joe, but Ellie was in a world of her own.

Waving bye to Flora as she left, Mr Gimbal made his way back into the centre. The children were free to explore the village, hoping Mr Iam would come very soon.

The sun glistened down on the water of the swimming pool as they walked beyond the centre. Passing the bowling green, tennis court and empty football pitch, there was a quiet stillness in the air.

"Everyone must be working and only have activities after work," said Ellie.

Joe agreed as they sat on a wooden bench. Ellie took the tokens from her pocket. Just as Joe had predicted, there were only two.

"I did tell you to look after them," said Joe, passing Ellie a tissue to dry her eyes. As they enjoyed the warmth of the sun, Joe felt a hand on his shoulder. He turned to see Mr Iam. As he sat next to them, there was a reassuring calmness.

"You faced your fear to overcome, you passed that test and you have won. You both felt lost and all alone, not wanting to be on your own. But when you found the path to light, you knew that all would be alright. Before you start on number three, enjoy a fun activity. At Mr Gimbal's you must stay, before you head off on your way." Mr Iam passed a brown envelope to Joe. His arms stretched out to grip their shoulders. Joe and Ellie looked at his face, his kind eyes so bright for such an old man. If only he could make this journey with them. But, how could he? They would have to be brave and courageous. Before they knew it, he was gone.

Joe opened the envelope; glancing at the rules, he turned the card over as they read the next riddle:

> *"To solve the riddle, find the clue,*
> *you must follow what to do,*
> *ascending upwards you must go,*
> *to leave behind what's left below."*

"We're going to be flying on the feathers, I just know it," said Ellie, beaming.

Joe looked down at the riddle; his face said it all. "I knew we would have to face something to do with heights. I couldn't go through that again, like the way we arrived here," Joe said sadly.

"Well, neither could I. I don't mind being up high, I'll be with you," Ellie said, giving Joe a comforting closed-lipped smile.

*

Back at the centre, Mr Gimbal was just finishing up his work for the day. Hanging up his apron, he couldn't resist adjusting his feathers in the mirror, while Joe and Ellie crawled on all fours trying to find Ellie's missing tokens without success.

Sniggering behind a garden wall, he put them in his black waistcoat pocket. "Should have been more careful," he said to himself.

Chapter Eight

The Third Riddle

Walking up the path of the Activity Centre, the lights twinkled against the dark sky.

"Look," said Ellie. Joe and Mr Gimbal turned around as the illuminated giant feathers came floating in to land. Joe and Ellie watched excitedly as the Whodins each disembarked, blowing their whistles, sending the transportation on its way.

"I wish we had this at home, what an ace way to get to school," said Joe, beaming.

Mr Gimbal opened the door. "Right, make your way in," he said, taking off his jacket to reveal his pink tutu.

As they watched the Whodins approaching, Ellie spotted Purdy carrying some boxes.

"Hi Ellie, hi Joe," said Purdy, putting them down. The black and white cat-woman looked flustered.

"Are you OK?" asked Joe, concerned.

"Yes, just rushing, nearly forgot the boxes for Mr Gimbal, he needed some for storage. I run The Box Factory for Mr Iam. It's been busy today with deliveries of farm produce. Then our call to meeting, back to the factory, back here," she said, her furry face looking stressed.

"We'll help you with those," said Ellie, bending down to pick up the empty boxes.

As they made their way down the corridor, Mr Gimbal spotted them. "Ah, there you are." Taking the boxes, he led the children to the storeroom. "You can find some little people's clothes in the back of the cupboard by the overalls. Someone from the old factory made them for the others, but they left them behind. Right, must go, got to be ready for my dance class. You decide your activities and I will see you later on." Checking himself in the mirror, he closed the storeroom door.

"I've seen that place on the map, The Old Factory and The Box Factory, it's past Whodin Town, I think," said Joe, scratching his head.

"Where do you think the others went to, Joe? Where have they disappeared to?" Ellie asked anxiously.

"They must be somewhere," replied Joe.

"Maybe they got here like we did and didn't follow the rules, and they paid the consequences," said Ellie with tears in her eyes.

"Who knows, Mr Iam didn't say, but he knows everything going on, be sure of that." Joe and Ellie pulled the clothes out of the cupboard. "It smells like our Christmas decorations when they come out of the attic," said Joe as he wrinkled his nose, smelling them.

Joe headed straight to the large hall to find Mr Bun as Ellie wandered down the corridor, the walls echoing with voices, music and laughter. Peeping through the glass portholes, she spotted Clarissa playing her harp with a band. Flora was carrying a large pile of books towards the waiting readers. Artists were preparing their paints and easels, but she had only one activity on her mind.

"Right, stretch, stretch, stretch," commanded Mr Gimbal as the dancers held the pose towards the mirrored wall. Ellie squeezed between them, smiling at Purdy.

*

The bright sun burst into the room as Joe pulled back the curtains. Picking up his rucksack, he knocked on Ellie's door as he headed down the stairs.

"Beat ya!" Ellie boomed as she was tucking into her breakfast.

"You could have woken me," said Joe, rubbing his eyes.

Mr Gimbal placed a package on the table. "I've given you some football rolls, fruit and a drink each, that will keep you going," he said, sitting at the table with them.

"Thanks for having us," said Joe. "Hope we can see you again."

"Not a problem, yes, me too. Now you had better hurry and be on your way, I must go to work," replied Mr Gimbal promptly.

Joe took the whistle from his backpack as Ellie read the last riddle:

> *"To solve the riddle, find the clue,*
> *you must follow what to do,*
> *ascending upwards you must go,*
> *to leave behind what's left below."*

"Here goes," said Joe. Inhaling deeply, he blew the whistle hard.

"It's not coming," said Ellie, looking above the rooftops. "Let me do it." Ellie grabbed the whistle out of Joe's hand. "Like this," she said as she blew with all her might. But no feather came.

"This can't be right. I think we should go back to 'Which Way Crossroads', there's no other pathway through the village," suggested Joe.

Back at the crossroads, Joe got out the map. Ellie's cheeks were red from her efforts to call for transportation.

"It's climbing, not flying," declared Joe, reading the sign.

"Whistle Top Mountains, there," yelled Ellie, pointing on the map. "It says east is that way."

Joe held the compass. "Come on, let's go," he said. They headed along the open-wooded pathway.

＊

"Keep up, Winston, we don't want to lose them," demanded Caiden, his long, black, feathered jacket sweeping behind him.

"OK, Boss, how much further?" replied the exhausted little rat-man.

"I knew one of the others should have come, you're so unfit, you should have stayed in the village," Caiden said harshly. "You go into the town and find Douglas, see what you can get. I've got this covered." Winston's head looked to the ground as he turned around to head back, as Caiden watched the children in the distance, behind the tree.

＊

The hot sun was burning the back of his neck as Joe put on his baseball cap, wearing it backwards.

"Mum would go bananas, I'm not wearing sun cream," Joe said, wiping the sweat from his face.

Ellie flicked back her long blonde hair. "I need my drink," she said, as the route began to grow steeper.

Opening out into a meadow, the pathway faded beneath the long, swaying grass.

"Pretend this is the jungle," said Ellie, excited as it came up to her middle. "Let's be lions hunting their prey."

"If you like," said Joe reluctantly as Ellie waded through, lifting her arms up to roar. Reaching the other side, through the trees, the ground became stony underfoot as they looked for the pathway. The light breeze refreshed their pink faces.

"Look, you can see for miles, there's Activity Village down there, and the river," Ellie said, excitedly pointing.

Joe turned around, his feet unsteady on the loose stones. "Whatever, just, let's keep going, I'm not looking down," he said, firmly turning back quickly to regain his balance.

With the path levelling off, they looked for a place to have their picnic. Ellie waved her arms to shoo the insects away as Joe got their jumpers from the rucksack. The air felt much cooler now they were close to the top.

"I don't mind it here, it's just the steep, stony bits I don't like," said Joe. "My legs go like jelly and I feel like I'm going to slip."

Joe hadn't told anyone until now, not even Mum, of that dreadful day hiking with Dad in the Lake District. If it hadn't been for the trekking pole to pull him up, he might never have got out of there. His bruised legs had shaken, as he had lain for what had seemed like hours, until Dad had found him. He never wandered off alone again.

"We've nearly done it, Joe, only one steeper bit and we're there," Ellie said with encouragement.

As they headed back on the well-worn path, a group of hikers were heading towards them. Joe looked at their equipment: rucksacks, map, compass and whistle, and each was holding a trekking pole.

"That's the clue we need, a trekking pole, I'm sure of it," said Joe.

"Hi, guys, you've nearly made it, care to join us?" said Flora.

"Yes please, but we need to get our clue, though. Do any of you have it?" asked Joe, his expression resembling Grandad's dog, Sam, waiting for his biscuit treat. Flora opened her white daisy rucksack. Unfolding the trekking pole, she handed it to Joe.

"I knew it, thank you."

"You're welcome, let me introduce you to the others. This is Mr Grainger, he lives at the mill, he organises hiking and boat rides when we don't have to work. Mr Haywood, he runs the farm. This is Franklin—"

Ellie butted in. "You run The Token Bank."

"Correct, hey there," said the woolly sheepdog-man, shaking their hands.

Before Flora could introduce the others, Mr Grainger stepped in front. "We should get a move on, it looks like rain coming in, let's do it!"

Leading the way, the hikers headed to the last steep incline with Joe, Ellie and Flora at the back as the dark, misty clouds started to close in on them.

Chapter Nine

Whodin Town

Buttoning up the top of his coat, his hood sheltering him from the blasting rain, Joe focused on his every footstep following Ellie's as Flora walked behind him.

"Watch the rocks, it's slippery," shouted Mr Grainger. But with visibility quite poor, it was impossible to see properly.

Joe wiped his dripping face, his hands cold and wet as he steadied himself with the trekking pole, nervously climbing his way up.

"Not far now," yelled Mr Haywood, gripping on to Ellie's hand as they clambered the last few steps to the top.

"We made it!" declared Mr Grainger. The hikers headed towards the bothy to take shelter. The sun was now appearing from behind the clouds; the grey, murky sky faded, as the rain had stopped.

"I'm soaked!" Ellie bawled as she struggled to walk, her wet jeans sticking to her legs.

"We can dry off here and take a break," instructed Mr Grainger.

Handing them towels from the trunk in the corner, Franklin and Mr Haywood took the kindling from the wood pile to start the fire. Flora hung the wet clothes over the Pulley Maid to dry.

"That's a funny clothes drier," said Ellie, laughing, as Flora pulled the string so their wet clothes were hanging above the fire.

"My nan has got one of those over her cooker in the kitchen, but I don't think she uses it," replied Joe. Looking around the bothy, Joe spotted a sign on the grey stone walls. "What does that say?" he asked, his dusty, bare feet tiptoeing up to read it.

"Mr Iam's rules, don't you have them?" asked Flora.

"Oh, yes, we do, they are on the back of our riddles," replied Joe.

In fact, they were everywhere to be seen: on the wall of the kitchen at Mr Gimbal's, by the golden ladder at Clarissa's, in the hallway of the castle and in the corridor of the Activity Centre.

"We all live by Mr Iam's rules, it is the right way," said Flora. Everyone nodded in agreement.

"But what if you get it wrong sometimes?" Ellie asked, concerned.

"That's just it, nobody can get it right all the time, but if you are trying to, Mr Iam knows that. He does understand," Flora answered.

As the warm, glowing embers of the fire lit the stony, dim shelter, Joe inhaled the smell of crackling wood, a comforting reminder of his wood burner at home, as they all sat chatting and sharing the fruit Mr Grainger placed on the bare wooden table.

Tucking into her juicy, red apple, Ellie's eye caught something shiny from the logs beside the fireplace. Reaching down to pick it up, she held it in her fingers. "Look what I've found, it's the letter 'C' badge, just like Winston's and Caiden's." The bright silver letter shone prominent against the black background.

Everyone was silent, staring at each other, as Joe and Ellie waited for a response. Mr Grainger cleared his throat; taking the badge from Ellie, he threw it into the fire. "So, you have met some Collectors, I see," he said, his forehead wrinkling.

"So that is what the 'C' stands for, what do they collect?" asked Joe, holding out his hands expressively.

"The Collectors are all ones that chose to live by their own rules. They were all Whodins once, but gave up their rights to be one when they decided they would rather steal than work for a living. They want us to change and be one of them so they can gain control of the castle and Mr Iam, to take over ruling our land."

"So why doesn't Mr Iam get rid of them?" Ellie asked.

"Don't you see? Mr Iam lives by his rules, he wouldn't hurt them. He hopes they will come to their senses and choose the right way. They will never have the power he has, he created them. I think they will have to decide to come back eventually," Mr Grainger replied, clearing the table.

"So, they steal whatever they can for themselves, they don't earn tokens or use the Activity Centre?" questioned Joe.

"No, and they haven't got transportation either, so they have to walk, or sometimes they just take my boats to go down the river," Mr Grainger said sadly. "You have to watch, they are friendly but very sly. Everyone helps each other anyway, so we're OK."

What a strange place this was, with no electricity or proper transport, telephones or computers; but everyone seemed content, enjoying their work and play.

The sun dazzled as they left the bothy; shielding their eyes, they saw Mr Iam walking towards them. Joe and Ellie observed how happy they all were to see him as they shook his hand in turn. He had that magical presence about him, like that of Father Christmas.

"Joe and Ellie, I can see, little people come to me," said Mr Iam, reaching out his arms towards them.

Stepping forward, he bent down to shake their hands, a radiant smile on his bearded face.

Saying goodbye to the hikers, he led the children to the rocky look-out point. Joe unravelled the map as Mr Iam pointed out the places they had been to so far.

"Look, I can see your castle in the distance," Ellie said excitedly as it stood prominent beyond the mountain range and forests below. Joe breathed in the fresh mountain air, watching an eagle circling around.

"I don't feel scared anymore," he said openly.

Mr Iam put his arm around Joe's shoulder. "You faced your fears to overcome, you passed that test and you have won. Reaching new heights up to the sky, you thought that you were going to die. But following the one who leads, was really all that you would need. You're doing well but there is more, here is riddle number four." He handed Joe the little brown envelope, and with that he was gone.

"I wonder how many clues we have to get?" asked Ellie as they sat on the rock overlooking the valley.

"I dunno, but look what we have so far," replied Joe, getting the objects from his rucksack. "A torch, a compass with a whistle and now a trekking pole, all the things that you need for hiking."

"Can I read the next riddle?" Ellie asked, reaching for the envelope.

"Sure, I wonder what else you need?" said Joe, passing it to her, putting the clues back in his bag.

"To solve the riddle, find the clue,
you must follow what to do,
find the shop of Mr Bun,
something tasty for your tum."

"That's easy, bread or cakes, Mr Bun runs the bakery. You need food for a hike," Ellie stated, then smiled at Joe.

"There's Whodin Town down there, let's go," said Joe excitedly.

Joe blew one long whistle in the hope for transportation. Immediately, a giant white feather floated to the ground beside them.

"Wow! It worked, that was quick," said Ellie, amazed. Holding on to the little white handles for balance, they were hovering over the ground. "Tell it where to go," instructed Ellie.

"Whodin Town, please," Joe requested as the feather gained height. Floating gently on a breeze, they descended down Whistle Top Mountain.

"Woohoo, this is cool," shouted Joe.

Gliding over the treetops, the children spotted a waterfall cascading down the rocks and the river below.

"That must be Mr Haywood's farmland." Ellie pointed. Beyond Whodin Town were fields, with row

after row of something being planted. Skimming the top of the chimney roofs of The Old Factory and The Box Factory buildings, the feather began to make its descent beside the sign 'Whodin Town'.

"Where is everyone?" Ellie asked as they walked towards the centre. There was an eerie silence around, just the occasional dog barking and birdsong. Passing the row of shops either side of the street, everything seemed shut.

"There's Flora's," said Joe. Looking into the dark window of the shop, arrangements of flowers were everywhere. Her flowery sign was set above the little shop door.

"What's that tapping?" asked Ellie as they made their way further down the cobbled pathway, the sound becoming louder and louder.

'Tap, ta-ta-tap, tap, tap,' it repeated.

"It's coming from around the side of here. Look, The Token Bank," said Joe, pointing to the wooden sign above the large, black metal door. Walking around the grey stone building, they watched his feet tapping the beat.

Chapter Ten

The Token Tree

"You aren't gonna see it," muttered Winston. His feet were tapping the now-familiar sound. Above the drainpipe, across a high ledge, stood a red-haired fox-man. His bushy tail was swiping the air. Ellie grabbed hold of Joe's arm to pull him back, scared that they had been seen. As they slowly made backward steps, the fox-man's head turned towards them, his furry nose twitching.

"Joe and Ellie, I believe, you came just at the right time," he said in a slow, monotonous voice.

"Good to see ya," said Winston, turning, taking hold of their hands to shake. Climbing down the drainpipe, the fox-man came to greet them, brushing off the dust from his smart, checked waistcoat and trousers.

Joe gripped tight to his rucksack strap. This was their only way of getting back home; he would need to guard the objects with his life.

"Hi, Winston, and who are you? We haven't met before," said Joe nervously, looking at the fox. Joe couldn't help but stare at the shiny 'C' badge on his pocket.

"Douglas. Glad to bump into you both, we need your help."

Ellie peered from the back of Joe. "How can we help you?" Ellie replied, biting her lip.

"Well, Franklin has asked us to collect the tokens for him as he isn't working and all, so we were helping him out. If you don't collect from the token tree every light, then it won't come the next one," said Douglas.

Joe and Ellie looked puzzled. Why would Franklin ask Collectors to get the tokens? What was the token tree?

Looking down from the stony ledge, Ellie and Joe studied the glass-domed roof.

"So, there is a tree growing inside the bank," said Joe.

"Mr Iam planted it, it's a token tree. The water underground keeps it growing. You just scratch the surface of the soil and find the golden tokens. They are replaced every light. Then they are banked and kept until they are collected," Douglas answered. Douglas seemed to know all about The Token Bank. Maybe Franklin was testing him to see if he would do the right thing for once and want to change back to being a Whodin.

"They come out of the ground, then, that's awesome," replied Ellie.

"Yeah, Doug, you used to sometimes give me extra, you must have counted them wrong, but I'm not complaining," said Winston, laughing.

"Uh-huh," muttered Douglas, lifting up the manhole cover. "Franklin forgot his keys, so we have to use the other entrance."

Leading them down the steps into the tunnel, Winston turned on the light.

"This is an odd way to get in," said Joe. Ellie hung on to the back of Joe's rucksack, brushing away the dangling cobwebs.

"I don't like spiders, I want to get out," said Ellie, panicking.

As they reached the end of the large tunnel, small ones led off in different directions.

Joe brushed his hand across the damp soil wall. "How are you supposed to get the tokens from under the ground, then?"

Douglas shone his torch, lighting up a small, dug-out hole. "You just climb through there and when you come to the end, you scratch away at the soil, and the tokens appear."

Joe looked at the dark, damp tunnel. "How do you two fit through there? It looks too small," he said, puzzled.

"We, um, haven't dug out enough yet, hey," said Winston, his tail tapping the ground.

Joe looked around at Ellie. They didn't exchange

words, but their faces looked the same. This had to be a trap, and they had to get out.

"Sorry, but we can't crawl through there, can we, Ellie? I'm not a fan of small spaces and Ellie's scared of spiders, so we'll leave you to it. See ya, bye," said Joe bravely. Quickly grabbing Ellie's hand, pulling her, he started to run back down the tunnel. "Get out of here," he muttered as she hung on to him, dazed by his actions.

"Shame you couldn't help, your loss," Douglas shouted, his voice echoing as they scrambled up the steps.

Running back to the cobbled street, hanging on to each other, they looked for help.

"That looks like Mr Bun," said Joe, breathlessly pointing ahead. Chatting and laughing to his team members, he 'high-fived' them as they left. Joe and Ellie ran to meet him.

"Are you OK? You look a bit scared, was it the journey down? I didn't expect you yet," said Mr Bun, opening the door to his bakery.

"We are just glad to see you," said Ellie with tears in her eyes.

"You must be tired and hungry, come and freshen up, I've made the perfect supper."

Finishing off their last few mouthfuls, the little brown dog sat patiently looking at Joe, his tail wagging.

"Come here, Champ, you can have your supper now," said Mr Bun, shaking the box of food.

"I miss my dog, we walk him every day after school," said Ellie sadly.

*

"So that's how Douglas knows so much about The Token Bank, he used to run it when he was a Whodin," said Joe, curled up on the sofa.

Mr Bun nodded; Ellie enjoyed the cuddles from Champ as he sat on her lap.

"Mr Iam will know what they are up to, as he doesn't miss anything. They will give up one day. I know most of them miss something of their old life, especially those who played footy," said Mr Bun.

"I miss home – I love football and we might win this year. We need to get our clues so we can get back," Joe said, concerned.

"Oh, I nearly forgot about that," said Mr Bun, walking to the kitchen. Handing the tiny loaf of bread to Joe, he put it in his lunchbox. "This is made from a special recipe, made to last," said Mr Bun.

*

Joe inhaled the scrumptious, sweet smells of the bakery. "You have lots to do before the shop opens;

does everyone start work before light?" asked Joe, looking like he needed more sleep.

"The birdsong wakes us, then it's full steam ahead to bake all the bread and cakes, so that Octavia can make her sandwiches and rolls," said Mr Bun.

Ellie carried the finished tray of iced delights, her white apron dragging on the floor. With the counter now full, the shop was ready to be opened. Joe put the last few football rolls in the net basket.

"I'm going to bake cakes and decorate them for a job when I'm older," Ellie stated. "Mine will be ballet and dancing ones," she said, gliding her way to the sink to wash up.

The sound of a familiar voice was heard coming into the bakery.

"Well, if it isn't our little Joe and Ellie, busy, busy," said Octavia, smiling. The bluebird put her bread basket on the worktop. "Mr Iam is in the teashop. He said he was coming to find you both. I'll let him know you are here. Come and have a cup of tea and angel cake. It's just divine, toodle-loo." Waving her fingers, she collected the next full basket and left.

"Thanks for your help, guys," said Mr Bun, handing the children four golden tokens each. "You might find something to spend it on at the Shop of Surprises," he said, holding out his hand to 'high-five' them.

"What do they sell there?" asked Ellie, responding while putting her tokens in her unzipped pocket.

"That's it, you pay and get a surprise." Everyone laughed.

"I should have known that," said Ellie, her cheeks turning red.

"Thanks for letting us stay," said Joe. They said their goodbyes as they left.

Passing them the biggest slice of angel cake you could imagine, Octavia served them tea. The wooden table rocked on the uneven floor. In fact, the whole teashop had an old-fashioned feel. Like stepping into a 'once upon a time' sort of story.

*

"We just had to tell you," said Joe, feeling relieved that Mr Iam knew about what the Collectors were doing.

But he didn't look at all surprised. "You had to choose what's right or wrong. Your conscience to guide you along. To steal from others was their plan. But you chose right, you left and ran. You passed that test and you have won. There's three more riddles, then you're done." He pushed the brown envelope across the table and with that, he was gone.

Chapter 11

The Harvesters

*"To solve the riddle, find the clue,
you must follow what to do,
a healthy snack grown from the tree,
many of them you will see."*

Joe read the riddle to Ellie and Octavia.

"Something that grows from a tree. It must be fruit," suggested Ellie.

"Or nuts, maybe," said Joe.

"Well, well, you'll need to be on your way then," said Octavia, getting up from the table to clear away. "Must get back to work, lots to do."

Pulling the latch on the teashop door, the little bell rang. Waving goodbye to Octavia, the children headed through the town. Before they headed out to Mr Haywood's farmland, sure to find their healthy snack, they couldn't resist visiting the Shop of Surprises.

Gazing at the endless choice of items on display in the window, Joe opened the door. Peering head and shoulders over the counter was a little white mouse-lady.

"Little people, come in, take a look around. When you are ready, your surprise will be waiting."

Joe and Ellie wandered around the Aladdin's cave of goodies. Past the painted pictures of landscapes, a variety of wooden musical instruments, books, clothes, boxes with birds on and soft marshmallow chairs.

"How come we can't choose how to spend our tokens?" Ellie said, nudging Joe.

"I suppose the whole idea is that you like to have a surprise," he said, making his way back to the little white mouse-lady.

Putting his hand in the saw dust drum, Joe pulled out a small blue packet as Ellie gave the mouse her two tokens for her go. Ellie took hers, brushing the bits from her arms. Opening up the neatly sealed surprise, the mouse-lady watched in anticipation, as Joe uncovered a familiar-coloured pattern on three rectangular cards. Looking shocked, Joe turned them over, revealing three football players.

"What is it?" asked Ellie, frowning at Joe's discovery.

"Must be just what you needed," said the little white mouse.

"They are the cards I took from Ben Wilson's collection when I went to play at his house. He has so many packets every week. He was going to fill his book well before mine. I thought he wouldn't miss them," said Joe, embarrassed by his revelation.

"So, you stole them," said Ellie, raising her eyebrows. Like the look you might get from a grown-up when you get told off for doing wrong. Ellie opened her small packet to find a pink pencil sharpener in the shape of a horse. Looking at Joe, her cheeks grew redder as she revealed she had 'borrowed it' from Hollie in class and had meant to give it back.

"Enjoy your surprises," said the mouse-lady as they headed towards the door.

*

Finally, with the town behind them, and following the open pathway towards the farmland, after what seemed like ages, Joe was first to speak.

"As soon as I see him, I'm giving Ben Wilson his stickers back. I'd rather not have them than feel guilty about taking them. Cloud Land knows we are just as bad as the Collectors. I don't want to be like them," said Joe, cross with himself.

"Everybody does what we have done, Joe. Samantha Shelby takes sweets from the corner shop when no one is looking," replied Ellie sharply.

"But that doesn't make it right, it's all stealing. Cards, sharpeners, sweets, whatever, it's all wrong," said Joe. "How would you feel if it was your things that went missing?"

Ellie screwed up her face as if closing her eyes would take away the problem. "I know, you're right. I'll put it back in her drawer as soon as I'm back at school."

As they followed the signs to Mr Haywood's farm, the pathway took them past a field of sunflowers. Ellie revealed to Joe about the time when her dad's car was stolen outside her nan's house with all their shopping in the boot.

"I didn't get to bed until midnight and the police had to take us home. They found our car damaged and all the shopping was gone," said Ellie sadly.

Joe turned the riddle card over to look at Mr Iam's rules: '3. Don't take anything that isn't yours'.

"Everyone should follow this," said Joe, turning it over again.

Opening the white picket gate to the farm, Joe and Ellie looked across the flat green landscape as the warm sun shone down. In the distance stood row after row of fruit trees, with people busy going up and down ladders, picking the fruit.

"They smell delicious," said Ellie, bending down to pick some strawberries from the row of plants.

"No!" shouted Joe. "You can't take them."

But Ellie wasn't having any of it, stuffing her face with the sweet-tasting fruit. There was every kind of fruit and vegetable you had ever seen, all growing at the same time.

"That's strange," said Ellie, her mouth a bright shade of red. "Every time I pick one, a flower appears in its place." Sure enough, the strawberry plants' flowers were growing amongst the fruit.

Joe and Ellie watched as the people worked hard to pick the produce, and all by hand.

"You can see how everyone gets fit. They don't have any farm vehicles, just like the old days," said Joe.

But this was nothing like the old days. The repeating whistle sound filled the air as they watched the transportation come and pick people up with their full fruit baskets, heading towards The Box Factory.

*

"I'm sorry, Mr Haywood, I didn't think," apologised Ellie as they finished eating their salad rolls, handing him her apple as a gift.

"No worries, Ellie, but you must try to live by the rules. Don't take anything that isn't yours," he said.

Joe took the riddle from his pocket. "Please can we have our clue? It will be growing from one of your trees."

Leading them through the rows of vines, he picked a bunch of red grapes. Joe put them in his cool box as Mr Iam appeared.

Ellie gripped on to Joe's arm, afraid. "Sorry, Mr Iam, I shouldn't have taken the strawberries," she said, her voice quivering.

But he just looked at Mr Haywood, and then smiled at Ellie as if it was all OK.

Leading them out to the edge of the vineyard, Mr Haywood walked with them as Mr Iam reached the end of the picket fence.

"So, all the Whodins who work for you are harvesters? It's hard work picking all day," said Joe.

"Well, every light, there's more to pick again, it never ends. But sometimes things are different. When the rain comes, and doesn't stop, the fruit rots, with too much ground water. The weather seems to be changing." Joe and Ellie looked at Mr Iam, and for the first time his face looked a little troubled.

"New produce grows at every light, and everything was going right. But there is change upon my land, nothing I can do with my own hand. As heavy rains begin to fall, and we don't see the sun at all."

Joe took his library book from his backpack and handed it to Mr Iam. "We have been learning about climate change in school. This will tell you why you have had this happen, because our land, Earth, is causing it."

"You have to do something to change that, then," said Mr Haywood, looking at the book.

"Yes, we all must," said Joe.

"Guess what? I've got a good idea. When we get back home, I'm going to tell our school council we should all write to Parliament. See if they can do more to stop it," suggested Ellie.

Joe nodded.

"I want to read and take a look, at what is in this special book," said Mr Iam, clutching the cover.

"Sure," said Joe.

"Thank you for telling us what's wrong, now to help you along. I'm trying to build a wind machine, that will fulfil your dearest dream. To send you home the way you came, back down to Planet Earth again. So, solve this riddle, and find the clue, and you'll only have one more to do." He handed them the little brown envelope. With that, he was gone.

"You don't know how much this has helped us to know why our crops have been failing sometimes. If Mr Iam could have done something, he would have," said Mr Haywood, shaking their hands.

"So, what has happened to the little people who were here before? If they haven't been seen and Mr Iam hasn't made a wind machine to get them back home, where are they?" questioned Ellie.

"There is talk that the Collectors are holding them, but no one really knows. Everyone keeps away from Dark Forest. That is where their den is. They are fine when in small groups, but not all together. You have already met Caiden, he's the one who started this rebellion," said Mr Haywood.

Saying goodbye, the children closed the white gate as they looked to the forest beyond.

"I'm scared to open the envelope," said Joe. "Why do I have a feeling we'll be heading through Dark Forest?"

Chapter Twelve

The Collectors

The buzzing bee sound hummed in the air as they sat in the long, grassy meadow.

"Read it, Joe," said Ellie, impatiently getting the map out of his rucksack.

Joe tore open the envelope:

> *"To solve the riddle, find the clue,*
> *you must follow what to do,*
> *keep listening for a rippling sound,*
> *and what you need is all around."*

"It's got to be running water, that's it," said Joe confidently. "Think about it, we have bread and fruit, and you need a drink for a journey."

"I think you're right," said Ellie, opening up the map. As they looked at it, the river flowed from Whistle Top Mountains valley, through the farmlands and wound its way through Dark Wood. Then back around near Whodin Town and Activity Village, past the mill and granary near Mr Iam's castle, and beyond.

"I think we're meant to find the river through Dark Wood, or else why would Mr Iam lead us out away from the farm?" said Joe anxiously.

"What if the Collectors have kidnapped the other children and they can't escape? Maybe they are slaves, we'll be next," said Ellie as she began to cry.

"We don't know that. They don't seem to be nasty to anyone. They want to get the Whodins on their side, so they can rule. They are lazy and greedy, that's all. Without the powers that Mr Iam has, how can they rule?" said Joe, rolling up the map.

Following the well-worn footpath, the giant fir trees shaded them from the sun as they headed deep into Dark Wood.

"If we keep on this track, it looks like it will bring us alongside the river. We can fill my drink bottle up with some water there," suggested Joe.

"OK, I wish these things would stop biting me," replied Ellie, scratching her arms.

Joe breathed in the mossy pine air as he pushed back the overgrown fern on the path. "Can you smell a bonfire?" The smoky wooded aroma grew stronger as they approached an opening ahead through the trees.

"Yes, it must be the Collectors' den," Ellie replied nervously. "Let's go back." But they knew they had to go on.

The pathway was visible the other side of the wooden shack as the campfire smoke rose up above the trees. Just then, a fair-haired, thin woman appeared from the doorway, and following her was Caiden.

Joe and Ellie crouched down in the undergrowth, afraid of being seen. Trying to stay silent, they watched as fear gripped their faces. A woman, with the features of a squirrel, was carrying a tray of mugs and handing them out to Douglas and Winston as more people joined them.

"There are lots of them," whispered Ellie, gripping tightly to Joe's arm.

Joe gestured for her to be quiet as Caiden began to speak.

"I can't hear what he's saying," Ellie muttered as the burning campfire crackled.

"Something about the call to meeting and a drawbridge. Must be to do with the castle," replied Joe, putting his finger to his lips.

Just then, the Collectors raised their mugs in the air, shouting. "Here's to Caiden, one and all. Take what you want, don't work at all. We don't follow Iam's rules. Only Whodins are the fools. We're Collectors, here to stay. We won't live the Whodin way." There was a loud cheer as they sat back down around the camp.

"We will have to wait until they go back inside," suggested Ellie as the Collectors sat chatting.

But Joe came up with a different plan.

Slowly and quietly, they crept around the perimeter of the grounds, keeping well out of view. Almost in the clear, and about to join the pathway the other side, Ellie screamed at the sound of the loud horn for a call to meeting.

"Ellie and Joe," shouted a voice from the crowd as Caiden got up to run to them.

"Leg it!" screamed Joe as he gripped Ellie's hand.

The narrow dirt pathway was the only escape. Ellie's screams filled the air as Caiden fast approached them.

"I can hear water," panted Joe, breathless as they reached the rippling sound. Tied up on the riverbank was a small, wooden boat. Releasing the rope, they quickly dragged it to the crystal water's edge, climbing in as Caiden grabbed an oar.

"Wait, I want to speak to you," shouted Caiden as the currents pulled the little boat downstream.

"I hate water!" hollered Ellie as Joe glanced back at Caiden, his black, feathered arms waving frantically at them.

"Just hold tight," said Joe, trying his hardest to keep control. He missed the prominent rocks as they floated downstream.

With forest either side of the river, Joe began to guide them to safety.

"That was close. Don't worry, when we get to a clearing, we'll try to head for that and get off," said Joe.

Ellie hung on to the handle at the side, watching the clear water flow. "I can't swim yet, I don't like my head in the water."

"Hopefully you won't need to," he replied, using the oar as best he could.

With the forest now behind them, the river widened, flowing more calmly as the open grassland stretched beyond the horizon.

Stepping onto the dry riverbank, Ellie's legs shaking, they pulled the boat with all their strength, tying it securely around the trunk of a tree.

Clambering up onto the grass, Joe took out his drink container. "Well, I've filled it with water, it has to be the right clue."

"I can't tell you how scared I was. You did really well," said Ellie, laying back on the grass, exhausted. Resting in the warm sunshine, Ellie passed Joe her drink. "I hope Mr Iam comes soon."

Leading the way, Joe opened the gate to the adjoining field. "If they find the boat, they will be on our tracks. I think we are safer to keep moving." In the far side of the field, harvesters were working the land as the whistling sounds brought the transportation. "That's a relief, Whodins, the meeting must have finished," said Joe happily.

Mr Iam appeared, heading towards them as the children ran to meet him.

Joe took the object out of his rucksack. "I hope this last clue is right," he said, holding his bottle of water.

Mr Iam took it in his hand in front of them. "Water, the drink I choose first. Sipping often, you won't thirst. Yes, you have now got the clue. Getting it was hard to do. Through the dark, Collectors' den. Back onto the path again. With Caiden following your trail. You faced your fears and did not fail. Water is your friend not foe. It took you where you had to go. You passed that test and you have won. There's only one more, then you're done."

Joe put the drink back in the rucksack.

Ellie grabbed Mr Iam's arm. "Have you managed to finish building the wind machine yet?" she asked, concerned.

"Just trust that soon it will be done. To end your game and say, 'We've won!' Your land should cause the wind to blow, and then I can just let you go."

Ellie and Joe smiled as they shook his hand, thanking him. He took the little brown envelope from his pocket, smiling as he gave it to Joe. With that, he was gone.

"We're nearly there, Ellie, just one more riddle and we've finished the game," said Joe excitedly. "I can't believe that all this has happened to us and my dad is still in the park, as if time has stopped."

"Yeah, so my family will still be on the beach waiting as well," commented Ellie. "I hope it works, what if we can't get back?" she said, frowning.

"Of course we will, we've nearly done it. We've faced our fears and told some truths, why shouldn't we?" replied Joe.

But was it enough? Would Earth send the wind? What if the wind machine didn't work? What if they just couldn't get back home and had to stay in Cloud Land forever? Joe opened the envelope and read the riddle:

"To solve the riddle, find the clue,
you must follow what to do,
this last clue will unlock a door,
you'll find it in a bluebird's drawer."

"A bluebird's drawer, Octavia is the only bluebird we know," said Ellie.

"Looks like we are heading back to Whodin Town, then," said Joe, happily.

Chapter Thirteen

The Last Riddle

The orangey-pink sky of the setting sun made their journey unforgettable as the giant feather came into land. Ellie blew the whistle, sending it back up the mountains as they headed to the bluebird's teashop. Walking through the cobbled streets, pretty-coloured lanterns hung on the light posts as they reached the town square.

"What's going on?" asked Ellie.

"Let's go and ask them," replied Joe as they walked towards the people hanging bunting over the shop doors and windows.

"It's a celebration, we are getting ready for a big party. News has come that a Collector has decided to come back to us. We must get ready to welcome them," said the man excitedly.

"Who is it?" asked Ellie enquiringly.

"We don't know yet, but Mr Iam has been here to give us instructions. They will return with him at dark."

The town square was a hustle and bustle of activity as the Whodins prepared for the party.

"I wonder if we know them?" pestered Ellie.

"I don't know, but we had better find Octavia first. I have a feeling they will be needing our help before we can get our last clue."

*

The little bell tinkled as Joe opened the teashop door.

"Joe, you made it. Ellie, come in. We will talk later, but first there's lots to do. Please can you carry these?" Octavia asked, passing the children a tray each of sandwiches.

"Told you so," said Joe, raising his eyebrows with a smile.

The banquet was ready as Flora finished putting the flower decorations on the table. Mr Bun placed the white iced cake in the centre.

Octavia led the children through the back door of her kitchen. Handing them the wicker basket, they followed her.

"Pick as many as will fit in the basket, everyone deserves a sweet treat. I'll be back in a mo. Toodle-loo," she said, leaving.

Joe and Ellie stared at the unusual tree sprouting honeycombs from the branches.

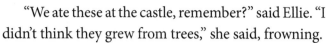

"We ate these at the castle, remember?" said Ellie. "I didn't think they grew from trees," she said, frowning.

"They don't, but they do here, just like there's a milk lake," he said, surprised. With the basket full, they headed back to the square. Octavia and Mr Bun carried the rest of the plates and napkins.

"Clarissa," shouted Ellie as she ran towards the beautiful lady. Her long, white dress was dazzling like diamonds.

"Hello, Ellie, hello, Joe," she said as Joe approached her. "How are you getting on with your riddles? Have you got all the clues?" she asked in a soft, gentle voice.

"Just one more and we will have done it," replied Joe with a smile.

"It has been lovely seeing you, but I do hope you get back home," she said as she turned to set up her harp for the music.

Joe and Ellie looked to find Octavia as coloured lights flickered against the dark sky. Across the square, she stood directing the Whodins where to be seated as the town filled with an air of excitement.

"You two, woohoo." She beckoned, her other hand on her hip, as the children went towards her.

With everyone seated and chatting, quietly waiting, Joe leaned over to Octavia.

"We have our last riddle and the clue is in your drawer," he said with anticipation.

"Yes, yes, I know, but first we have a welcome back celebration, that is very important to us. You will stay with me and, at first light, we will get up to find your clue."

Joe thanked her as the loud horn sounded. Everyone stood up, clapping and cheering as they looked up. The white landing lights flashed in the distance as it approached the town. The crowd grew louder as Ellie put her hands over her ears. Mr Iam stood, blowing the horn as the feather came to land on the stage in the centre. The crowd fell silent, sitting and waiting, for Mr Iam to reveal the identity of the person in the hooded, black cape.

"He chose to go it his own way, tempted he was led astray. To live a life that was not right, he followed darkness not the light. A Whodin he was meant to be, by choosing now to follow me. He said I'm sorry for what I've done, we forgive you, welcome home Winston." Mr Iam removed the cape as the pink-eared, rat-man, dressed in a shiny, gold suit and shoes, tap-danced before them. Pausing, he shouted, "Good to see ya!"

The crowd of Whodins stood again to cheer, clapping as Mr Iam stood with his arm around him. Clarissa and the band started to play as Mr Gimbal, Purdy and the dancers joined them on stage.

The rat-man smiled as tears rolled down his face. "It's good to be home, Boss," he said, looking at Mr Iam.

Mr Gimbal skipped his way to the front in his pink, feathery tutu. "Right, let's party!" He gave two short claps as the dancers joined him.

Winston did a tap dance as Mr Iam applauded, smiling. With the party in full swing, the air was filled with laughter and music.

"I'm stuffed! I couldn't eat another thing or I think I might be sick," said Ellie, the evidence covering her face.

"It's been nice to see everyone again," said Joe. "I'm glad Winston chose the right way to live at last. He seemed pleased that Mr Grainger is giving him his old job back."

"Yeah, he looks happy being a Whodin. But you know what that means, Caiden, Douglas and the others will be really angry. I hope we don't have to see them again," replied Ellie, frowning nervously.

Waving goodbye with tired faces, the children made their way back to the teashop.

The wooden stairs creaked as Octavia led them up into the small attic.

"I've made the beds all clean for you. Now you need lots of sleep, we need to be up at first light." Hugging them, she waved her feathery blue fingers, closing the latch of the old wooden door, shouting, "Toodle-loo," as the stairs creaked. The moonlight shone through the tiny porthole window as Joe and Ellie slept.

*

"Cup of tea?" came the voice, opening the door. The teapot rattled as she placed it on the dresser. Sitting on Joe's bed, she pushed back her blueish-black, slept-on hair. Ellie started to wake as Joe was sat up, his rucksack spilling all his belongings.

"The riddle said our last clue will unlock a door, you'll find it in a bluebird's drawer. That must be a key we need," said Joe, holding the card. Octavia nodded. Passing them china cups of warm, purple tea, Joe inhaled the strong aroma. "Blueberry, my guess," he said, turning to Octavia.

"Well, yes, of course. The finest ones grown by Mr Haywood," she said proudly.

"What door will it unlock?" asked Ellie in a yawning voice.

"Well, well, that is for Mr Iam to reveal, you just need the clue." The sunlight beamed through the small, round windowpane.

"I'll prepare breakfast while you freshen up, then we must be going."

Leading down the cold, stony steps of the cellar, Octavia pressed the light button. Ellie winced as she stepped, avoiding the dusty cobwebs. The musty, damp smell made Joe shudder.

"Our cellar is cold like this," he said, folding his arms. Dragging the table and chairs across the room, she lifted the patterned, dusty rug as they watched, engrossed. Hiding beneath, was a bronzed, metal hatch. Sliding the bolts open to lift it, the heavy door groaned. Joe and Ellie peered down the open black hole.

"You will need your torch," said Octavia as Joe unzipped his rucksack. Shining to find the light button, Octavia pressed it. One by one they descended down the metal ladder rungs, following Octavia. There in the middle of the stony walled vault was a tall chest of drawers.

"Ah, great, which drawer will it be in?" asked Joe excitedly.

Octavia looked at them, her feathered face concerned. "Unless you can unlock the code, we won't know," she said, pointing to the combination lock at the back.

Chapter Fourteen

The Kite Children

"How do we know what the code would be?" asked Ellie, looking puzzled.

"What I want to know is, why is the key locked up like this?" said Joe, looking to Octavia.

Her deep black eyes flitted around, as if avoiding the question asked. "No one from Cloud Land knows about this secret vault. The key was placed there by Mr Iam. Only he knows the code for your drawer, and the codes for the objects in the other drawers. None of them managed to get past this part of their game."

"Who didn't? What are you talking about?" said Ellie, grabbing the bluebird's arms.

"Do you mean the other little people that have been here before? We thought the Collectors were holding them hostage as slaves?" said Joe.

Octavia paused, as if thinking hard at what to say. "The kite children that came before. Some of them didn't get this far, and the ones who did couldn't work out their code. No, the Collectors don't have them. Everyone thinks they do, but you see, they are waiting. Waiting for someone to come who does finish their game, because only then, will they be allowed to be sent back home."

Joe and Ellie's mouths fell open in surprise.

"So, where are they, then?" asked Ellie.

"In a secret place of the castle. Mr Iam and I look after them, in the hope that the wind machine will be completed and someone else will come to play and finish their game. Then you both arrived."

"But why can't they just live with the Whodins until someone else came?" Ellie enquired.

"They would reveal too much about your world. You are not made like us. Our land is very different to yours. If it was not kept a secret, then everyone would want to access the castle grounds, and try to find a way of reaching the portal you entered through. No one can pass the drawbridge except Mr Iam, kite children and me. You see, I was the first one he made. I am the castle key-keeper." Joe and Ellie looked at each other, then looked back at Octavia.

"We must work out our code," declared Joe.

Ellie placed all the objects on the floor in the order they had been given them as Joe looked at the combination lock.

"There is every letter of the alphabet on here, can you see a letter on any of the clues? I hadn't noticed anything before," said Joe. They both studied the objects, revealing nothing.

"How will we know what our code is, then?" Ellie asked, getting upset.

Joe took the riddles from his pocket. "Wait, there's a letter on every riddle in the top right corner."

Using his pad and pen, Joe wrote down the seven letters in order. "F-a-r-i-m-e-e, farimee, that isn't a word," he said, puzzled.

"Yes, but what can it make?" said Ellie, grabbing the pen.

Octavia smiled, watching the pair working it out.

"I hope this is right," said Joe, pressing the letters on the combination lock. 'I-a-m-f-r-e-e'. The middle drawer pushed open. "Woohoo! We did it, it was right. I am free, we are free, Ellie," Joe said as they jumped up and down in excitement, holding each other.

Octavia took out the ornate silver key. "Well done, both of you," she said, passing it over to Joe. "Now we must be going, Mr Iam will be waiting."

The giant feather came to land at the edge of the castle grounds as Joe, Ellie and Octavia stepped off.

"Mr Iam will be pleased you made it," said Octavia, leading the way. Joe bent down to tie his undone laces as his rucksack vanished before his eyes.

"Hey, my rucksack, come back," he shouted as the dark figure ran into the woods. Joe fled, chasing the culprit, as Ellie and Octavia ran after him, following the well-worn pathway. "Give it back," shouted Joe. With the thief still in view, suddenly the air sounded with one continuous blowing horn. Ellie gripped on to Octavia's hand, hard, as they tried to catch up with Joe. Reaching the stile, Joe watched as the black-caped figure sprinted across the field with his rucksack. Clambering over breathlessly, he ran with all his might as they headed towards the mill. The sound of the horn blasted and the Whodins approached, transported by the giant feathers. They descended, circled the field, and surrounded the dark figure.

"The Whodins have come to help us," puffed Ellie, climbing over the stile.

The thief stood motionless as they all walked towards him.

"Give it back, Caiden, it's no use to you," said Flora, holding out her hand as Joe, then Ellie and Octavia arrived. Joe stood facing Caiden as the black feathered man removed his hood.

"You can't keep running away forever. Your land was made for good, not bad. So was ours, and it's spoilt by people who make the wrong choices. But you are the one who can save Cloud Land," said Joe, bravely reaching out his hand.

Caiden was silent, looking at the Whodins around him as he passed the rucksack back to Joe.

"Thank you, you have helped us too," said Joe as Mr Iam approached them.

Caiden looked towards him with a stony-faced expression.

"Caiden, I would like to spend some time with you. So, we can sit and talk things through. But it's your choice, you must decide. To meet with me or run and hide."

Taking Joe and Ellie by the hand, he led them back towards the castle as Octavia followed. The all-familiar sights of the gardens surrounded them. The bright, white pillars and grey turrets dominated the blue skyline as they followed the path through the trees and around the pool.

Joe stood on the white glass island in the grassy ocean. The blades of the wind machine were held still in its silver metal frame.

"You finished it, then," he said, looking at the contraption in front of him.

Mr Iam pulled back the lid on the top.

"But what did we need the key for?" asked Ellie, standing next to Joe.

"The key unlocked your door to fear, and now it's gone, no longer here. As you were brave to play your game, you will never be the same. For facing it, you'll fear no more, because you chose to lock that door. Your game is over, and you won, for now you're free, you've overcome. Please give the objects now to me, to send the wind and set you free."

Joe looked at Ellie and smiled. "We made it, now we can go home." The children laughed, jumping up and down with excitement and hugging each other.

Joe passed the objects from his rucksack, as Mr Iam placed them one by one into the machine, closing the lid. Turning the large handle on the side, the blades began to rotate slowly.

"Look, there are the other kite children with Octavia," shouted Ellie.

In the distance of the garden, they watched the five children heading towards them, each holding a kite.

Mr Iam leaned down to face the children, a warm smile on his face. "Goodbye, Ellie, goodbye, Joe, now it's time to let you go," he said as he passed them their kites. Turning the handle once more, the blades quickened as the wind began to blow.

Unravelling their kite strings, Joe looked across to Ellie. "You did well, we both did," he said proudly.

"I couldn't have done it without you," she replied, her eyes welling up.

Octavia and the children were approaching the glass ground as the white cloud descended like a

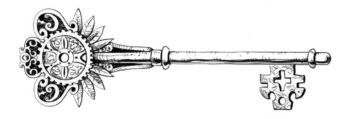

blanket around them, the wind blowing stronger and fiercer. Ellie's screams filled the air as they began to spin around.

"It's too late," shouted the voice. "They've already gone."

*

Swirling, twirling, spinning, Joe hit the ground with a bump.

"Are you alright, Son? I thought I was going to lose you," said Dad, shaking.

Joe opened his eyes, the cold air making him shiver. "So, did I, Dad, so did I."

Arm in arm, they stumbled back down High Point, heading for the car as Joe reached into his back pocket. Reading Ellie's address on the folded piece of paper, he put it back.

"Mum is never going to believe this," he said.

About the Author

Amanda Humphries has lived in rural Shropshire all her life. Married, with two grown-up children and a grandson, she worked for many years in a primary school as a H.L.T.A. teaching reception. It was her love of reading stories to her class that has inspired her to write her own books.

 Matador